Shoo, Fly!

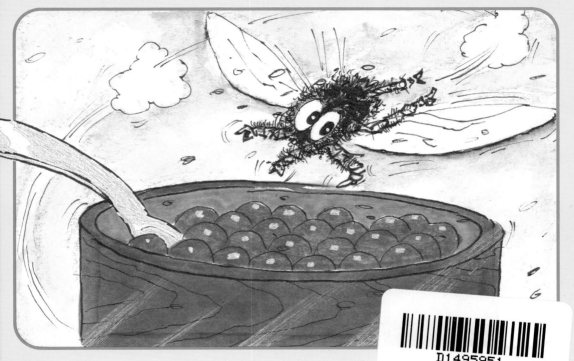

Story by Joy Cowley
Illustrations by Fred Ooms

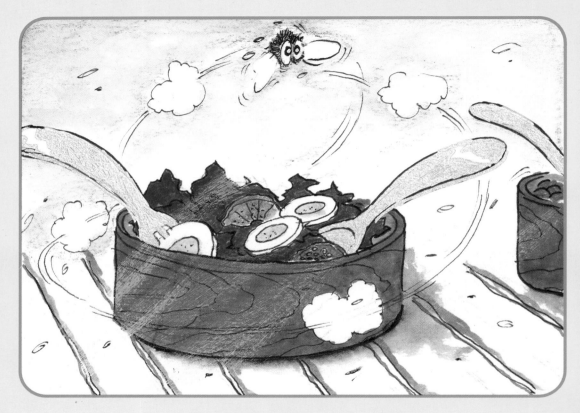

Around the salad.

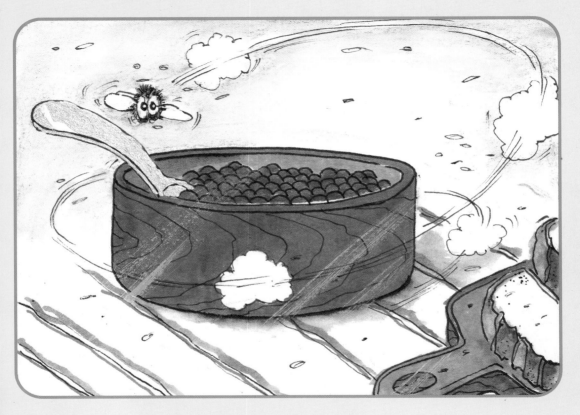

Around the peas. 3

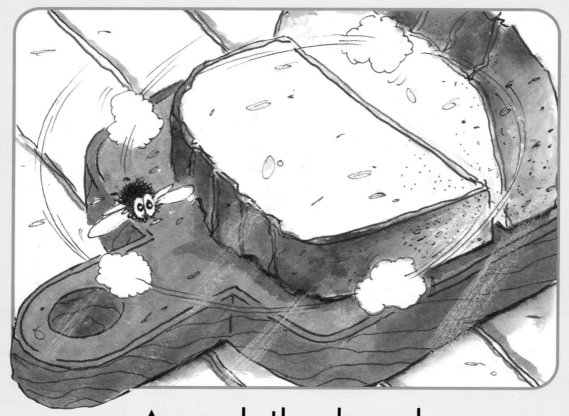

Around the bread.

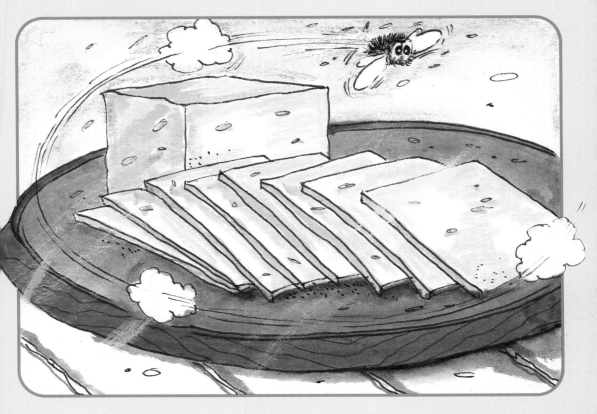

Around the cheese. 5

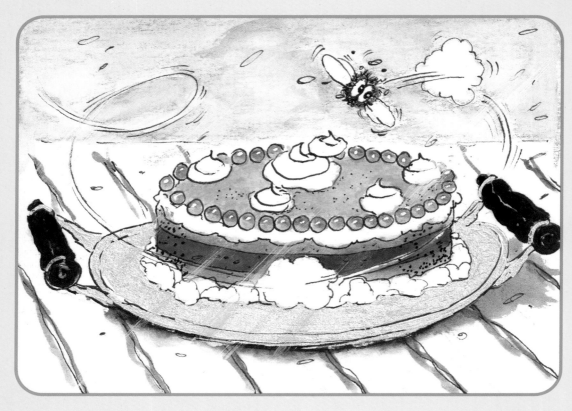

6   Around the cake.

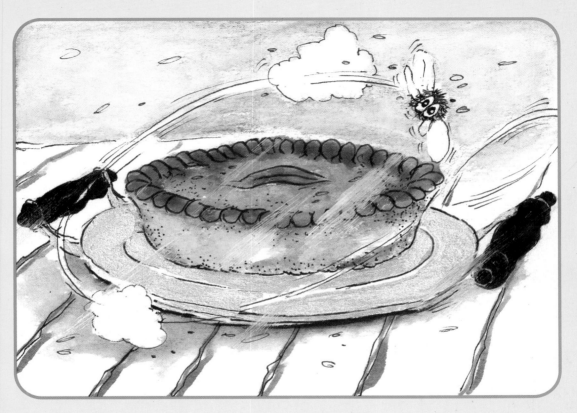

Around the pie.

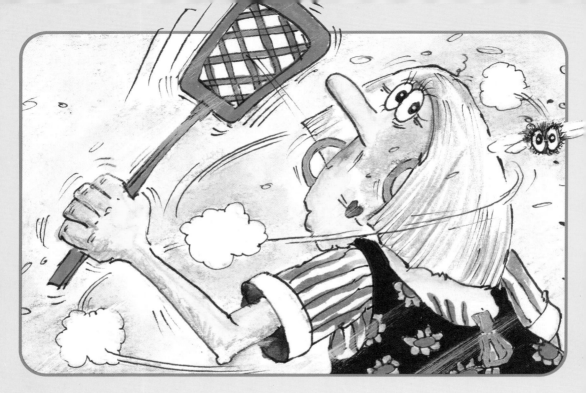

Around the woman.
"Shoo, shoo, fly!"